THE

WORST

SLEEPOVER

IN THE

WORLD

For dearest Tilly, who hates soy sauce.
And for Liv, her Mama, with huge love. — S D

To the family Ramos-Butterworth Sánchez — L L

First published 2021 by Walker Books Ltd, 87 Vauxhall Walk, London SE11 5HJ • 10 9 8 7 6 5 4 3 2 1 • Text © 2021 Sophie Dahl • Illustrations © 2021 Luciano Lozano • The right of Sophie Dahl and Luciano Lozano to be identified as author and illustrator respectively of this work has been asserted by them in accordance with the Copyright, Designs and Patents Act 1988. • This book has been typeset in Futura Light Condensed • Printed in China • All rights reserved. No part of this book may be reproduced, transmitted or stored in an information retrieval system in any form or by any means, graphic, electronic or mechanical, including photocopying, taping and recording, without prior written permission from the publisher. • British Library Cataloguing in Publication Data: a catalogue record for this book is available from the British Library • ISBN 978-1-4063-8441-3 • www.walker.co.uk

THE WORST SLEEPOVER IN THE WORLD

SOPHIE DAHL   illustrated by LUCIANO LOZANO

WALKER BOOKS
AND SUBSIDIARIES
LONDON · BOSTON · SYDNEY · AUCKLAND

Gracie was coming to stay the night. Gracie is my best friend. It was our first ever sleepover.

We talked about it all week, Mum, Ruby and me. Ruby is my sister. She's five. She and Gracie would sleep in my room with me. Gracie is seven and so am I.

Ruby and I planned
the midnight feast
we would have,
EVERY
night before bed.

Ice cream sundaes, crisps and flying
saucers, chocolate buttons and bootlaces,
milkshakes and cupcakes and pizza and donuts
and a chocolate fountain and lemonade and cola
cubes and lollipops and jelly-beans and chips
with mayonnaise for starters...

...but Mum heard and said we could have:
crisps and sandwiches and popcorn.

SPOILSPORT.

We were going to make a den,
read stories, and stay up all night.
We were going to dance like wild things,
and play, "Would you rather?" and
throw putty, high up on the ceiling. It was
going to leave marks like slug trails,
and no one would tell us off.

It was going to be...

THE BEST SLEEPOVER IN HISTORY.

On Saturday evening Gracie's mum dropped her off. She was going to a party. She had red lipstick and glittering shoes. Mum told her she looked beautiful. Neither my mum, nor Gracie's mum have a mum any more, so they help each other.

Mum made sausages and chips and broccoli for tea, and Gracie said: "I don't like sausages, I don't like THESE chips, and I definitely don't like broccoli."

"Oh," Mum said.

"I'm quite fussy, you see," Gracie said. "But I do like rice."

So Mum made Gracie a bowl of rice. "Would you like soy sauce?" she asked.

"Absolutely no thank you," Gracie replied. "I hate soy sauce, it's all brown and saucy."

After tea, we made some houses out of magnetic tiles and Gracie told us about a magic unicorn with a wounded hoof that lives on her roof, and then Mum said, "Would you girls like a bubble bath?"

So we squashed into the bath and everyone's elbows and knees were jabbing each other and it didn't feel that bubbly or comfortable, but it was exciting, because next, was the actual sleepover bit.

We went downstairs in our pyjamas and made the midnight feasts to put in our lunchboxes, with a spare one for Gracie.

Gracie didn't like cheese sandwiches. Or sandwiches at all. Not bread, or cheese, or crisps, so she had bread sticks and peanut butter for her midnight feast.

"This midnight feast is pretty boring," she said, staring accusingly at the bread sticks.

Mum told her she could have some pineapple to jazz it up.

"I don't think pineapple is very jazzy," Gracie sighed.

Mum laughed. "Well, my darling, I used to be out dancing on a Saturday night. Jazzy is what you make of it."

Upstairs, we made a nest of duvets and quilts and blankets on my floor, and we lay like a row of tin soldiers with our midnight feasts next to us, and the dog plonked herself in the middle and began to snore. My night-light shone stars on the ceiling. It was going very well. It was going to be the best sleepover in existence.

Then the dog made a terrible, pungent stink. We couldn't figure out which part of the dog made it.

"It was her bottom end!" Gracie shouted.

"Top!" I said.

"Just the dog's general, stinking being," Mum groaned.

"Yuck," Gracie said. "The dog is the Captain of Stench Town."

Mum aired all the blankets, opened the window, and wafted the hideous smell away.

7.45 PM We read Mum a story.

8.05 PM Mum read us a story.

8.25 PM We ate our feasts.

8.29 PM Gracie said she was starving.
Could she have a rice cake?

Mum trudged off downstairs…

and came back with a plate
of buttered rice cakes.

"I don't like butter," Gracie said.

Mum took a very long, deep breath.

"Sorry. I did tell you I was fussy,"
Gracie told Mum.

"You did," Mum laughed.

The three of us lay still on the floor,
looking up at the stars. It was quiet.

Gracie said that the floor was too hard and floor-y. She said she wanted to sleep in a bed. MY bed. I wanted to kick something. Someone.

"I don't want Gracie to sleep in my bed," I said. "It's my bed."

"I know," Mum replied, "but she is our guest."

Gracie got into MY bed. MY Mum tucked her in. It was outrageous.

"I don't like this sleepover," I said.

Mum rubbed my leg.

Ruby nodded. "Yep. I don't like it either."

"I absolutely love it," Mum said.

"Do you know that a rocket flew to space and exploded," Gracie announced.

"Were there people in it? Did everyone live?" I asked. I felt worried.

Mum cut in. "Why don't I sing you a lullaby?"

"And once, we saw a pigeon who was half squished but still flapping on the driveway and Daddy said, 'look the other way children and then…'"

"Golden Slumbers…" Mum sang, loudly.

"I have a tummy ache, a backache and a headache," Gracie said. "Could you put on some music? I don't really like singing."

Mum's eyes shone in the dark. They are big and green. She scrabbled to put the radio on. She knocked my Match Attax cards over.

"Do you have music with birds and oceans and rivers?" Gracie asked. "Because that's what I like. Kind of, yoga music?"

"I don't," Mum said. "But I'm sure I can find some, I'm a resourceful woman."

9.28 PM Mum played music from eight different radio stations. None of them had bird music.

There was crackling and violins. Gracie asked her why she couldn't just find some relaxing music on her phone? Mum said this was a good idea, and that she'd forgotten she had a phone. Her hand was on her forehead.

The phone music wasn't birdy enough, Gracie decided. We tried another playlist and it had a lot of ocean, but not enough birds. Another sounded like some seagulls fighting in a storm. They squawked in the thunder.

Mum got the giggles.

"I don't really feel **that** comfortable at this sleepover," Gracie said.

"Neither do I!" I groaned. "I want my bed back!"

Gracie ignored me and carried on talking.

"At the one other sleepover I had, Bella's sister stared at me while I was sleeping… and it was so creepy it woke me up. Then, she was sick on my leg."

"That sounds like a disaster," said Mum.

"THIS is the disaster," I said. "The worst sleepover there ever was."

"It's not great," Ruby agreed. She started crying, and…she fell asleep, mid sob.

"I think I've crushed my knee-bone," I yelled. "I think I NEED to be in my bed, URGENTLY. Either bed or the HOSPITAL. I have a leg injury. Not that anyone cares."

10.48 PM Mum had her head in her hands. The bird music was now crickets, and they sounded quite angry.

"I don't like those crickets," Gracie said. "They sound cross and sinister. They feel like they would look like Bella's little sister, if they were staring at your face in the middle of the night."

"I don't like them either," I agreed. "Gracie, just tell me, why are you in my bed?"

"I don't know why I'm here at all, actually," Gracie whispered. "I hate sleepovers. They're the worst. I might need to have a shout, a roaring shout; one that will wake up all the neighbours and pigeons..."

Gracie opened her mouth VERY wide...

"Ok!" Mum sang, in a loud, bright voice. "I think we need a change of plan! Gracie, would you like to sleep in my bed?"

Gracie smiled in the dark. "Oh yes!" she said.

"Ramona," Mum asked, "you can either get into your bed, or join Gracie in my bed, which would you rather?"

"I don't want to sleep with Gracie," I said. "She's not really my friend any more, with her pigeons and shouting and bed stealing."

Mum took Gracie to her bed. Gracie began to tell Mum a story of a lonely mouse with only one leg and no family.

"It's sleepy time, Missy." Mum spoke firmly. Then she tucked Gracie in and gave her a kiss.

Mum came back to my room. I hated Gracie and Mum.

"You love Gracie more than you love me!" I croaked.

"Crikey," Mum laughed.

"I love you so much, Ramona. Gracie's mummy's not here: I'm trying to make her feel safe and comfortable. Come and get into my bed too."

"No," I said. "Because you have your new daughter, Gracie, in there."

Mum cuddled me in my bed, in the dark.

"This is all going to feel so much better in the morning," she said.

"It won't," I replied. "This will NEVER feel better. THIS is the worst sleepover in the entire world. The worst in the universe and every galaxy, I think. Even undiscovered ones."

11.56 PM THE WHOLE HOUSE WAS ASLEEP.

I woke up in my own bed. The sun was coming through the curtains. I could smell coffee, and something delicious, from downstairs. I went to Mum's room and Gracie was sleeping in Mum's bed, with our dog and the cat. It made me laugh. Gracie sucks her fingers when she sleeps. It's actually so sweet. Ruby came in. She looked panicked.

"I went to sleep in your room but woke up in mine!" she said. "Call the police!"

Ruby, Gracie and I went into the kitchen. Mum was flipping pancakes. She looked a tiny bit tired.

"Good morning, lovely ladies," she said. "How did you sleep?"

We drank hot chocolate with whipped cream. We told her about Henry at school who says he can do wrist burns so hard they set your actual arm on fire.

"He sounds like a peach." Mum took a big gulp of coffee. "Another pancake, Gracie?"

Gracie smiled. "Yeah. I love pancakes," she said, dreamily. "I love your house too. Can I come again next Saturday?"

"I'll think about that!" said Mum.